GIRLS SURVIVE

Girls Survive is published by Stone Arch Books
a Capstone Imprint
1710 Roe Crest Drive
North Mankato, Minnesota 56003
www.mycapstone.com

Cataloging-in-Publication Data is available on the Library of Congress website.
ISBN: 978-1-4965-7853-2 (library binding)
ISBN: 978-1-4965-8013-9 (paperback)
ISBN: 978-1-4965-7858-7 (eBook PDF)

Summary: Twelve-year-old Ann understands there is only one thing to be
grateful for as a slave: having her family together. But when the master falls
into debt, he plans to sell Ann and her younger brother. Ann is convinced her
family must run away on the Underground Railroad. Will Ann's family
survive the dangerous trip and make it to freedom?

Designers:
Heidi Thompson and Charmaine Whitman

Image credits:
AFBPhotography: Alan Bradley, 112; Capstone: Eric Gohl, 108;
Shutterstock: ekler, 108 (inset), Max Lashcheuski, Design Element

Printed and bound in Canada.
PA47

ANN
FIGHTS FOR FREEDOM

An Underground Railroad Survival Story

by Nikki Shannon Smith

illustrated by Alessia Trunfio

STONE ARCH BOOKS
a capstone imprint

CHAPTER ONE

Eastern Maryland
Wednesday, November 15, 1854
Sundown

Ann shivered. The cold was everywhere.

The dirt floor of her family's one-room cabin was almost as cold as the November air. Earlier the sun and hard work in the field had kept her warm, but now Ann had to move closer to the cook fire. It didn't help. She would have to wait for the fire's warmth to fill the cabin.

"Ann, don't get too close, now," said Mama.

Ann pulled her feet back just enough to put Mama at ease.

Mama was a strong woman who always said her children were the most important thing in the world. She said no matter what Master Adam thought, they were *her* children, not his. Just because they were slaves didn't mean he owned their hearts or their souls.

Daddy always said Mama had a fire burning inside and that it was where she got her strength. But the fire inside Mama was burning out. It had started two months ago when Granny died. Mama barely ever smiled now, and she never hummed while she cooked anymore. Losing her mama had broken her heart.

Ann missed the old Mama even more than she missed Granny. If she had one wish, she'd bring Granny back to them. That way Mama would come back too.

Daddy sat down on the ground next to Ann and let out a groan, the same way he did every night.

His back was tired. Their family had spent all day pulling dried cornstalks from the hardened soil in the field.

Paul sat down where he didn't fit—right between Ann and Daddy. He was only five, and he couldn't stand to be more than three feet from somebody. He was scared of everything too. Maybe that's why he couldn't let himself be alone.

"Ann," said Mama, "hold the baby." Mama handed baby Elizabeth to Ann. As soon as she did, Elizabeth started to cry.

"She doesn't like me," said Ann.

Daddy laughed. "She doesn't like anyone but Paul and your Mama."

Mama sighed and said, "She misses Granny."

Elizabeth had been born during the last apple harvest, in early fall. She was twelve years younger than Ann. Two weeks later, Granny had died from an infection.

When Daddy came into the cabin the day after Granny died, he had found the baby screaming in one corner and Mama crying in the other. Ann hadn't known what to do so she'd sat by the fire with Paul and stayed out of the way.

Daddy had gotten Mama and Elizabeth calmed down and asked Ann to come outside to the garden with him. He had looked at Ann with a serious face.

"Ann," he'd said, "do you remember what Granny always called you?"

Ann had nodded. "She called me an old soul."

"Granny was convinced you'd been here before," Daddy had told her.

Granny had always said things that didn't make sense to Ann. "What does that mean, Daddy?" Ann had asked.

Daddy had chuckled and put his hand on her shoulder. "It means you're an old lady in a little girl's body."

Ann liked the idea of being like a grown-up, but not the idea of being an old lady. She had tried to figure out why Granny thought that, but Daddy had interrupted her thinking.

"You're going to have to be grown-up and help your mama," Daddy had said.

Ann had nodded again and followed Daddy back inside—and she had spent the last month or so trying as hard as she could to keep her promise to Daddy. If Mama needed help, Ann would help her.

So Ann held the baby, even though it was her least favorite job. It was a job nobody could do right, and Ann liked to do things right.

Elizabeth squirmed and hollered. "Shhh," said Ann. She bounced Elizabeth a little bit, like Mama did, but it didn't work.

Finally dinner was ready. Mama gave everyone a strip of pork and a piece of ashcake. Then she took the baby back from Ann and sat down.

Dinner in their cabin was almost always quiet. By the end of the day, Daddy was too tired, Mama was too sad, and Ann was too hungry to talk. Paul always had something to say, but someone usually shushed him.

Ann stared off while she chewed on her ashcake. She loved the way the sweet cornmeal taste broke through the ashes from the fire that covered it. Something in the corner of the cabin caught her eye—a spider!

Daddy said Ann was as brave and steady as any grown man he'd ever known, but she was afraid of spiders. "Daddy," she whispered. "A spider."

Daddy sighed. "Where?"

"Over there!" said Paul. "I see it."

Paul was trying to act like he was being helpful, but Ann knew better. He wanted Daddy to get the spider just as badly as Ann did. Paul didn't like anything that crawled. During tomato season,

he had to pick the worms off the crops, and he cried
the whole time he did it.

The only reason he did it at all was because he
was more afraid of the overseer than the worms.
The overseer watched the slaves' every move while
they worked in the fields, and he was mean.

When Paul had turned four and was big enough to help in the fields, he had seen the overseer whip Daddy. There was a lot to be afraid of on this farm, and bugs were the least of them. Sometimes Ann heard the older slaves talk about running away from Maryland. They said up north they could be free.

"Get it!" yelled Paul. He pointed at the spider.

"Shhh," said Mama.

Daddy groaned again as he got up. He walked over and squished the spider. "I don't know how you get through a day's work," he said. "Nothing but bugs in the fields."

Ann didn't answer. Outside she did what she had to do. Inside she felt safer. Inside she could ask Daddy to get a spider. Inside she could be a child.

After dinner Ann and Paul got into their sleeping spots. They slept on the ground on a small bed of hay. They lay halfway between the wall and the fire. Mama didn't want them to get burned, and they didn't want to be next to the cold cabin walls. The walls were made of logs, and the evening chill snuck in through the spaces.

Paul always scooted closer to Ann before he fell asleep. Sometimes she rolled away. Tonight his warmth felt good, so she let him stay close.

Paul started snoring about three minutes later. Mama sat up and nursed the baby, while Papa rubbed his feet and stared at the fire.

Ann always fell asleep watching her parents. She liked for them to be the last thing she saw every night and the first thing she saw every morning. She knew a lot of slave owners sold people away from their families. She never forgot to be grateful that hadn't happened to hers. Her eyelids began to feel heavy.

Just then, Ann thought she heard somebody whisper her daddy's name: "John."

Mama said, "Did you hear that?"

The voice came again, from outside the cabin. "John. You awake?"

Ann was wide awake again. No one ever came by this late. All the slaves turned in early, because they were all afraid to oversleep. If they weren't in the field at sunrise, they might be beaten.

Daddy got up and disappeared through the door. Ann heard whispers outside, but she couldn't hear the words. She looked at Mama's worried face and had a feeling her own face looked just as worried.

When Daddy came back in, his face drooped.

"John, what is it?" asked Mama.

Daddy squatted down and put his arm around Mama. He didn't answer her. Instead he stared at the baby. A single tear rolled down his cheek.

Mama stood up and faced him. "What?" she asked again.

Daddy looked at where Ann and Paul slept. Ann shut her eyes, so he'd think she was asleep too.

"Bad news," said Daddy.

Ann's heart sped up. She hoped nobody had died. She was just getting used to life without Granny. Ann held her breath so she could hear Daddy better.

"Daniel said that Sarah overheard Master Adam talking in the big house," said Daddy.

Ann liked Daniel a lot. He was Daddy's best friend. He lived in the cabin next door and his wife, Sarah, cooked for Master Adam's family.

"What did he say?" asked Mama.

"He's come on hard times. Money's short," said Daddy.

Mama started to cry. Ann didn't understand why Mama was this upset about Master Adam's money. The silence went on so long Ann opened one eye to see what her parents were doing. Daddy had his arms around Mama. Elizabeth was in between them, fast asleep.

"Who?" asked Mama.

To Ann, it seemed like a strange thing to ask. Did somebody take Master Adam's money? Maybe Mama and Daddy were worried one of them would be blamed.

Daddy whispered, "Ann and Paul."

Mama crumbled to the ground. Daddy caught the sleeping baby as she fell. Mama's whole body shook. "Not my babies," she said. "Not my babies."

Us? thought Ann. *We don't even know where Master Adam keeps his money.*

Ann watched her parents through one eye. Daddy got down next to Mama and rubbed her shoulder. Mama jerked up onto her knees. She put her face so close to Daddy's, Ann thought they were going to kiss.

"You have to do something. You can't let him sell my children," said Mama.

CHAPTER **TWO**

Eastern Maryland
Wednesday, November 15, 1854
Late night

Ann's eyes popped open. She strained to
hear her parents' voices over the thundering sound
of her own heartbeat. Master Adam had never sold
anyone away.

Why is he picking us? Ann wondered.

She thought if you did what you were told and
worked hard, you could stay with your family. She
thought slaves got sold when they caused trouble.
Daddy had taught her to follow the rules. He said it
would keep her safe, and she had believed him.

Anger and fear rose in Ann's body until her cheeks felt hot. She struggled to stay still. She wanted to interrupt, but she also wanted to hear the rest of what they had to say.

"There's nothing I can do," said Daddy.

Mama's face twisted with sadness and rage. "You can't let him sell the children. He picked them just because they're small and can't do as much work."

"Maybe he'll sell me instead," said Daddy. "I'll ask tomorrow."

Ann didn't want Daddy sold either. None of them could be sold. Ann always listened to the old people when they talked. She knew about places much worse than here. Places in the South. Families who were separated never saw each other again. None of them could end up somewhere like that.

"No," said Mama. "You can't ask. We have to act like we don't know. We have to make a plan."

Daddy looked at the ground. "They're going to two different farms. We only have till next week."

Ann couldn't take it anymore. She sat up and wiped her tears. "We have to run away," she said.

Mama and Daddy stared at her. The only sounds in the cabin were of Paul snoring and the fire crackling. It was like they were afraid to move . . . afraid that the words Ann had spoken would make the ceiling fall in.

After what felt like hours, Daddy handed the baby back to Mama and walked over to Ann. His voice was so low Ann almost couldn't hear it at all. "We can't run," he said. "They will hunt us, and you don't want to know what they'll do when they catch us."

"Then we can't let them catch us," said Ann.

Mama's eyes moved from Daddy's face to Ann's face as they talked. She swayed from side to side with Elizabeth in her arms.

"It would be too hard with the baby," said Daddy. "We could get hurt or sick. We could end up dead. All five of us."

Mama started to cry again. Ann knew being separated would blow out the last little bit of fire Mama had inside. *Not* running away might kill her.

"Please," said Ann. "We have to try. Some people make it. I've heard men in the field whisper about them."

Daddy shook his head.

"*Please?*" Ann could not imagine life without her family.

"That's enough," said Daddy. "I said no."

Ann lay down on the straw and turned her back to Daddy. Anger as hot as fire grew inside of her. It was like she suddenly had all of Mama's fire, plus her own.

Ann worried about being sold all night long. She thought about Paul all alone somewhere else. Every time a carriage came and went, she wondered about the world outside the farm. But she thought she'd never get to see it. Now she was going to see it in a way she never imagined.

When the horn that called them to work sounded in the morning, Ann hadn't slept. She thought about being sold while she yanked cornstalks from the ground. *I'll be sold next week*, she thought. Today was Thursday. Next week was only four days away.

Ann tried to think of a way to make somebody not want to buy her. If she got hurt in the field, she wouldn't be able to work. Then no one would want her. Even though Ann was strong and fast, she was small. Maybe the buyer would think she was too weak to do any work. And Paul was even smaller than she was. Ann hoped no one would want two skinny kids.

But Ann knew that plan might not work. If she was hurt, Master Adam would think she was useless and he'd sell her anyway.

On Friday night, Ann decided to talk to Daddy again. She waited until Paul fell asleep. They all knew Paul couldn't find out yet. He talked too much, and he'd be too scared.

"Daddy, we need to run away. Next week is almost here," she said.

Daddy stared at Ann. "I can't put you all in that kind of danger."

"What about the Underground Railroad?" she asked.

Ann didn't know a lot about the Underground Railroad, but she knew what it was from listening to the adults around her. She also knew what it wasn't. It wasn't under the ground, and it wasn't even a train. It was a secret path that slaves used when they ran away.

Along the path there were secret places to rest and get help. If you made it all the way, you'd be in the North. You'd be free.

"Leave it alone, Ann. You hear?" said Daddy. "I'm done talking about it."

Mama came around behind Ann and unwound one of her braids. She put in a fresh braid, and pulled it extra tight. She repeated this five more times, until Ann's braids were so tight her scalp hurt. Whenever Mama was restless, she redid Ann's braids. Usually that helped to settle her. This time, it didn't seem to work. Mama went outside in the dark and pulled the weeds in their little garden plot.

"Daddy, you told me to help Mama," Ann whispered. "Look at her. She can't watch us get sold. She just can't."

Daddy said, "Go to sleep. Now."

Ann knew better than to argue. She lay down next to Paul and stared at the ceiling and wondered if next week would come fast or slow. No matter what, next week was coming.

Ann was so upset she could barely breathe. The baby started crying. Since Mama was still outside, Daddy picked Elizabeth up and sang her a song, but she cried anyway.

Ann turned on her side and cried too. She couldn't believe her own daddy was just going to let her be sold without doing anything at all.

CHAPTER **THREE**

Eastern Maryland
Saturday, November 18, 1854
Midday

On Saturday, Ann noticed the field workers
sneaking looks at her and Paul. Every time she
looked at them, they looked away. They all had sad
expressions on their faces. Everyone's shoulders
slumped a little bit more than usual.

The workers in the field sang a song about the
Lord calling them by the thunder, and their voices
carried the heaviness of their hearts. The sadness
was heavier than any load of wood Ann had ever
carried.

Ann wished that instead of singing everyone would tie up the overseer so she and her family could escape. The overseer nodded like he was satisfied with the singing. To him, it meant that all was well on the farm.

Across the row from Ann, Daddy bent over and pulled a cornstalk. Daniel worked next to him.

"John," whispered Daniel, "what y'all gon' do? Run?"

Ann waited for Daddy to answer, even though she already knew what he would say. Daddy shook his head. "Too dangerous," he said. The two men never broke the bend-pull-toss rhythm of working the cornfield as they talked.

Ann waited for Daniel to try to talk Daddy into running, but he didn't say another word. She wished there was a way to stop time right in the middle of that night. Then she and Paul could stay with their family where they belonged.

If time were stuck, a Saturday night would be the best time for it. Usually Ann loved Saturdays, because after the work was done they'd have a break. There was no work on Sundays.

On Saturday nights, most of the slaves snuck to the woods beyond the farm and brought food to share. They'd eat sweet potatoes, greens, hog jowls, and whatever else people had saved up. One of the old women would tell stories of Anansi the spider and how he tricked everyone.

After they ate, someone would play the drums, or even a mouth harp, and people would dance. The children ran all over the place chasing fireflies. Even though nobody ever forgot they weren't free, they could pretend for just a little while.

That night, even though everything was about to change, they got ready for the gathering the same as always. Just before they headed for the woods, Mama said, "You all bundle up tonight. It's cold."

Ann and Paul put on extra layers, but Mama
urged them to put on more.

"Mama, that's all we have," said Ann. She
thought Mama must be trying to take extra good
care of them for their last days together. Ann already
had on two dresses. Paul wore his only pants and
two shirts.

"It's mighty cold," said Daddy. "Wrap up your
feet too." Since they didn't have shoes, this was how
they kept their feet warm in the winter. Everyone
wrapped up and bundled up. Mama even put extra
cloth around Elizabeth.

Mama gathered what looked like all of
their food, both rations from Master Adam and
vegetables from the garden, and wrapped it up in a
cloth. She tied the ends to make it easy to carry.

The Saturday party was just like it always was,
but it didn't feel the same to Ann. It was the last
Saturday party she'd ever have.

She sat and watched everyone. She tried to memorize every face and the words to every story and every song. She studied the dancing. She left the food on her tongue longer than normal, so she would remember the taste.

Paul sat right up under Mama and ate his food. He listened to the stories and laughed at the men trying to get women to dance with them. Ann knew that her little brother had no idea that his life was about to change forever.

"Time to head back now," said one of the older women.

Everyone collected their things and began heading back to the farm. Mama moved slower than usual. Daddy hugged Daniel tight and patted his back. By the time Mama was finished gathering their leftover food, everyone else was already out of sight.

Daddy bent down in front of Ann and Paul. "Listen," he said. "We're heading north. Right now."

Ann's eyes bulged. "We're running away? On the Underground Railroad?"

"Shhh," warned Mama. She looked around to make sure no one was there.

Daddy nodded. "I can't bear to see you get sold. A family belongs together."

"Sold?" asked Paul. "Who's getting sold?"

Daddy took both of Paul's hands. "Nobody."

Ann wondered what had changed Daddy's mind, but she didn't ask. All that mattered was that they were leaving together.

They stood in a huddle as Daddy told them everything he knew about the Underground Railroad and the trip north. Ann listened to every word he said. She knew he might need her help.

"We don't have a conductor to lead us north," said Daddy. "We'll have to find our own way."

"What's a conductor?" asked Paul. His voice was too loud as usual, and Mama shushed him.

Daddy said, "Those are the people who lead runaways to freedom and keep them safe."

Ann was starting to worry. If they didn't have a conductor, they might get lost.

Daddy continued. "I'm not sure exactly where to go, so we just have to keep heading north."

Mama's eyes got big. "John, you don't know where the first station is?"

Daddy shook his head, and Paul asked, "What's a station?"

"It's a place where runaways can rest and get help," answered Mama. Ann could tell from Mama's voice that she was worried too.

Daddy said, "We have to travel at night. It'll be scary, so you have to be brave."

"Scary?" asked Paul.

"Yes. But you can be brave, right?" asked Daddy. Paul didn't answer, so Daddy continued, "We'll have to hide a lot and listen out for pattyrollers."

"Pattyrollers?" asked Ann, looking back
and forth between Mama and Daddy. "What are
pattyrollers?" Neither one of her parents answered
right away, so she knew pattyrollers must be bad.

Finally Daddy said, "Pattyrollers get paid
to hunt escaped slaves and bring them back. They'll
hurt you if they have to."

Ann swallowed. People who got paid to hunt
other people were probably some of the meanest
people there were. She hoped they wouldn't hurt
children . . . or babies.

As if Daddy could read her mind he said,
"Just be quiet and stay close. I'll keep you safe.
But we have to go now."

Ann threw her arms around her daddy. He
hugged her tighter than he ever had. "Thank you,
Daddy," whispered Ann.

"There's no way I'm letting you two get sold,"
he said.

Ann smiled. Now Daddy stood tall and looked up into the night sky. Ann knew he was looking for the North Star. He put his finger over his lips to tell them to be quiet and pointed at the star. Then he motioned for them to follow him.

Ann's family headed north. Inside her chest, her heart beat strong like a drum, but she took a breath and remembered to be brave.

An owl hooted and Paul grabbed onto Mama's skirt. "Mama, are there ghosts out here?" he asked.

"Shhh," said Mama. Then she shook her head.

A mosquito buzzed in Ann's ear, and she swatted at it. Something scurried in the bushes off to her left, and something else screeched behind her. She thought maybe there *were* ghosts out in the woods. Just like she'd heard stories of Anansi, she'd heard stories of swamp ghosts who tried to lure people deep into the woods.

Be brave, Ann thought to herself.

As they walked through the black of night,
Ann felt the ground get soggier. Every step made
a sucking noise, and she cringed. Daddy had told
them to be quiet, but there was nothing they could
do about the ground.

Ann had to lift her feet higher, because the
grass here was taller. The moisture soaked through
the cloth around her feet, and she was glad Mama
had made her bundle up. Even in the dark, she could
see vines in the trees. Her questions about the world
outside of the farm were getting answered, and she
wasn't sure she liked it.

Ahead of her, Daddy stopped. "We're just about
at Greenbriar Swamp," he whispered. He looked up.
"At the first light, we'll have to hide."

Ann looked at Mama. Mama was worried—
it was all over her face. Still, Mama nodded and
followed Daddy when he walked again. Paul was
practically under Mama's skirt.

Thorns scratched at Ann's legs, and something much bigger than a mosquito buzzed past her face. She covered her mouth to hold in a yelp. Ann hoped it didn't get worse than this.

Just when Ann was about to ask Daddy if they could rest, he stopped. "We'll walk a ways in the swamp, so we don't leave footprints," he whispered. "Then we need to lie down in the grass all day and wait for night."

Lying in the grass seemed like a good idea to Ann. It would give her a chance to build up her courage again.

"I'm hungry," said Paul.

Daddy nodded at Mama, and she gave everyone a strip of pork to eat while they walked through the swamp. Ann felt something slither past her ankle in the muddy water and jumped. The splash scared Paul, and he squealed. Daddy glared at them and put his finger to his lips again.

The trip north was going to be harder than Ann thought. Right now she was causing more trouble than Paul. She would have to do better.

Finally, just before sunrise, Daddy moved to the edge of the swamp and found a spot for each one of them to lay in the grass.

When Daddy pointed to the spot for Paul, the boy whispered, "I want to hide with Mama."

Daddy pointed again, with a thrust of his arm, like he meant it. Paul sulked, but he lay down in his spot.

As the sun rose in the sky, Ann's family rested in the muddy grass. Ann watched big white birds fly silently in the sky above her. She could hear the soft sound of Paul snoring several feet away. She hoped nobody passing by would hear it.

Then she realized nobody would be passing by. They were in the middle of nowhere. Her bravery returned, and she let herself doze off.

The sound of baby Elizabeth hollering woke Ann up. She opened her eyes and off to the left, she saw a man with a big hat standing over Daddy. The hat was so big Ann couldn't see the man's face. Paul crawled to Mama, who sat up in her spot. Mama nursed the baby to keep her quiet. Daddy slowly rose to his feet to face the man.

CHAPTER FOUR

Eastern Maryland, near Greenbriar Swamp
Sunday, November 19, 1854
Midday

Ann watched Daddy stand up and hoped the
man didn't hit him. Daddy looked the man straight
in the face and said, "Afternoon."

"Good afternoon," said the man. He took off his
hat to scratch his head.

"Mama!" yelled Paul. "He's a Negro like us!"

"Hush," said Mama.

Paul knew how to act when the overseer was
looking, but when it was just the five of them, he
acted like he didn't have any sense. Ann wished she
was sitting with Paul so she could cover his mouth.

But Ann was surprised by the man's brown skin too. She was glad he wasn't white, but she knew he could still be trouble. He could tell on them. Or he could capture them and have them arrested.

"What are you doing out here in the swamp?" asked the man.

Daddy didn't trust many people, and Ann wondered if he'd tell the truth. But Daddy just stood there eye to eye with the stranger and didn't answer at all. They stood like that so long Ann thought maybe she should answer the man herself. She didn't want him to get mad at Daddy and hurt him.

Finally the man stuck out his hand. "I'm Nathan," he said. "I live over there. I'm just checking on my muskrat traps."

Daddy shook Nathan's hand, but he didn't tell him his name.

"You don't need to be scared," said Nathan. "Come with me."

Ann knew it didn't matter if Nathan was good or bad. There was nothing they could do but go with him. Daddy glanced at Mama nervously and motioned for them to come. They followed Nathan a short distance to a small house.

"This is my house," Nathan said.

A woman came to the door. "Nathan, who's this?" she asked.

"I don't know," said Nathan. "But I reckon they need our help."

The woman looked in all directions, then hurried them into the house. "Y'all are safe with us," she said. "Go on and sit down."

Mama's face relaxed. She sat down with baby Elizabeth in a chair near the fire. Paul sat on her lap, even though there was no room for him. Ann stood next to Daddy and waited to see what would happen.

Nathan pointed to the woman. "This is my wife, Mattie."

Daddy nodded at her. Finally he introduced himself. "I'm John. This is my wife, Beth," he said. He pointed to his children. "This is Ann, Paul, and baby Elizabeth."

Nathan said, "You running away?"

Daddy didn't answer, so Nathan kept talking. "I won't tell. Mattie and I are free."

Paul said, "You're *free?* You ran away too? Are we in the North?"

"Be quiet, Paul," said Daddy. Now their secret was out, thanks to Paul.

Nathan explained how he had saved up his money and bought his freedom, then worked until he could buy Mattie's freedom too.

While he talked, Ann looked around the room. The floors were wood instead of dirt, and they had a table to eat at. There were even a few dishes on a shelf against the wall. Ann noticed that both Mattie and Nathan wore real shoes.

She liked the way freedom looked so far. She imagined her family sitting at a table eating dinner.

Nathan smiled at Paul. "You're not in the North. Not yet," he said.

Daddy lowered his voice. "We'd sure appreciate any help you can give us in getting there."

Nathan sighed. "I don't know a lot about the Underground Railroad. We aren't a station. I don't know where to find one, but we'll do what we can."

Mattie said, "We'll feed you, and you can stay here until dark. I think I can give you some fresh clothes too."

Tears fell from Mama's eyes. "Thank you," she said.

Ann could see the trip was taking its toll on Mama. The circles under her eyes were darker than usual, and the corners of her mouth turned down. She looked like all that was left of her inner fire were embers. Ann wiped Mama's tears with her fingertips.

They all unwrapped their feet so they wouldn't get any more mud on Mattie's floor. Since they wore all the clothes they owned layered on top of each other, they peeled off their outside layers too.

Paul only had one layer on his bottom half, because he only had one pair of pants. They used to belong to someone else, and they were way too big for Paul. His shirt hung down to his bony knees.

Mattie gave them some possum stew. While they ate, Mattie took Paul's pants and cut the wet part off the bottom. They almost looked clean, and now they weren't too long any more. Paul put them back on and grinned at Mattie.

Mattie also gave Mama a pair of shoes and wrapped fresh cloth around Ann's feet. Ann wished this was the North so they could stay with Mattie and Nathan longer.

Daddy and Nathan talked in low whispers off to the side. Before long, it was dark outside.

"All right. It's time to go," said Daddy. "Nathan, Mattie, thank you for your help."

Nathan said, "Remember, go past the fields and keep going until you get to the Choptank River. Follow it north."

Daddy nodded. Nathan and Mattie stood outside and watched Ann and her family head back toward the swamp. In silence, they made their way north. They continued to walk for hours and hours. With a full stomach, Ann felt much better. The sounds of the night were less scary.

They kept a steady pace until Ann could smell mud in the air. Then she saw the river in front of them. The moonlight reflected off of the water. It almost looked peaceful.

They kept the river beside them and walked in the grass a long way. Finally Daddy crouched in the bushes and motioned for them to join him. They ate some ashcake and listened to the night sounds.

Daddy said, "When the tide starts to come in, we'll walk into the river. The tide will cover our prints."

Paul whined, "Daddy, how long till we're in the North?"

"I don't know," said Daddy. "Tomorrow's Monday, and the overseer will know we're gone when we aren't in the field. We need to get as far as we can before that happens." Daddy kept his pace and ignored Paul's sighs.

Ann was the first one to hear something rustle in the bushes. Whatever it was, it was big. It moved again, and Daddy motioned for them to all lie down.

Ann held her breath. The thing in the bushes moved again, and a stick snapped. They stayed as still as logs in the bushes.

Ann saw feet pass the bushes where she hid. Then another pair and another. They were not alone out here.

A voice whispered, "She said it was just west of the Choptank. Just go through where it branches off into a smaller river to get there."

"I don't see nothin'," said another voice.

"She said face the river, go straight across it, then keep going till we see the house," said the first voice.

There was a long silence, and Ann could see the three pairs of feet standing with the toes pointed toward each other. The people were standing in a circle. Suddenly one of the voices said, "Did you hear that?"

Ann's stomach tied in a knot. Elizabeth was making little grunting noises in the bush where Mama was hiding. The feet moved toward the bush.

Just in time, Daddy jumped out. The other people jumped back. There were a lot of shuffling noises, and one pair of feet ran off in the other direction. Someone whispered, "Run, y'all!"

Another voice whispered, "No. It's all right. It's more runaways."

Ann, Mama, and Paul stayed hidden in the bushes and listened to Daddy talk to the other voices. They were on their way to a station on the Underground Railroad. Ann couldn't believe it! Maybe her family could go to the station too. They talked so quietly Ann couldn't hear anything else they said.

After a while, Daddy whispered, "You all can come out of the bushes." Ann was the first to crawl out. Two men and a boy about Ann's age stood with Daddy.

Ann was full of questions. She wondered where the men were from. She wondered how long they'd been running. Most of all, she wanted to know how they knew where the station was and whether or not it was all right for them to bring along extra people.

When Daddy motioned for his family to follow
the men, Ann was relieved. Daddy put Ann on his
shoulders, and one of the other men put Paul on his.
The boy held Mama's hand. Together they made
their way across the small river.

Ann looked down from her spot on Daddy's
shoulders to make sure the water wasn't getting
deep, but it never rose above Mama's waist. The
sun was just coming up, but they could see a house
in the distance. Ann knew it had to be the station.
It was so close they would be there in no time. They
made it across and crouched next to the river.

The three strangers decided to keep going all
the way to the station, even though it was almost
daylight. Daddy decided to go with them to check
everything out first. Then at nightfall, if everything
was all right, his family would join him. Ann didn't
want to wait, but she didn't want to travel with the
sun coming up either.

Daddy said, "Beth, if this doesn't work out, get back to the river. Nathan said walk north in the water until the river disappears."

Ann, Paul, Mama, and the baby crept as close to the house as they could, then hid in the bushes. They watched the men walk. They all crouched down low, instead of walking tall.

As the men approached the house, Ann heard hoofbeats in the distance, and one word came to mind: *pattyrollers*.

Ann's heart thumped so hard it felt like it might burst through her chest. The men stopped in their tracks. They'd heard it too. They were closer to the house than the bushes, so they all ran forward.

Daddy slipped in the grass, and Ann fought the urge to yell for him to hurry. He fell behind the other men by several yards.

Go, Daddy! Hurry! Ann thought. She held her breath as the hoofbeats grew louder . . . and closer.

CHAPTER FIVE

Eastern Maryland, near the Choptank River
Monday, November 20, 1854
Near sunrise

Ann watched as Daddy struggled to catch up. She could no longer tell the difference between the hoofbeats and her own heartbeat. Seconds felt like hours.

And then Daddy made it to the house, just behind the other men. They knocked on the door and were let inside. Ann let out the breath she'd been holding. Next to her, Mama exhaled too. Seconds later a wagon came into view. It stopped in front of the house. A white man climbed down from the seat and knocked on the door.

Ann kept her fingers crossed, hoping he was one of the helpers on the Underground Railroad. Daddy had said some of the people at stations would be white. Ann and Paul had been surprised that white people helped Negroes hide, but Daddy had said, "Good *and* bad come in every size, shape, and color." If this man wasn't a helper, there would be trouble.

A woman opened the door, talked to the man for a little while, and then handed him a basket of something. They were too far away to hear anything, but the man nodded and left again.

Paul whispered, "Good. He's leaving."

After the wagon was gone from sight Paul asked, "Mama, can we go to the house now too?"

"No," whispered Mama. "Your daddy said wait until dark."

Ann knew darkness was a long way off. The sun had just come up. Mama gave them another piece of pork and told them to lie down after they ate.

Now that she was still, Ann realized all the muscles in her body were tired. They had walked two nights in a row. Their rest had been cut short yesterday when Nathan found them. She lay down and let herself fall asleep.

When Ann woke again, it was dusk. Paul was staring at her. Mama and Elizabeth were sound asleep. Paul pointed at Mama and then pointed toward the house. Ann knew he wanted to go be with Daddy. She shook her head at him. Paul was going to have to learn to be patient. The sun wasn't even all the way down yet.

As soon as it was dark, Mama woke up. It was like her body had told her it was time. The four of them crouched in the bushes and watched the house for a while. All was quiet.

Mama said, "Ann, you go first. Paul, you follow Ann. I want to be in back so I know I'm not leaving anyone behind."

Ann nodded. Without Daddy to take the lead, it was her job to help Mama, and she would not fail. She couldn't fail. She crept out of the bushes so carefully the leaves barely rustled. She looked at the house. It seemed like the lantern on the porch was welcoming her.

A wagon must have gotten there while they were asleep, because Ann hadn't noticed it before. She looked back at the bushes. Paul peeked at her, and she motioned for him to come on.

But just as Paul came out of the bushes, a bunch
of shouting came from the house. The door opened,
and a man with a gun made two of the runaways
from earlier get on the wagon. Another man came
out, pushing the boy along.

Ann dove back into the bushes and watched in
horror as slave catchers forced their three friends
onto the wagon. The man with the gun guarded
them, and the other one went back in. There was
more hollering . . . and a gunshot.

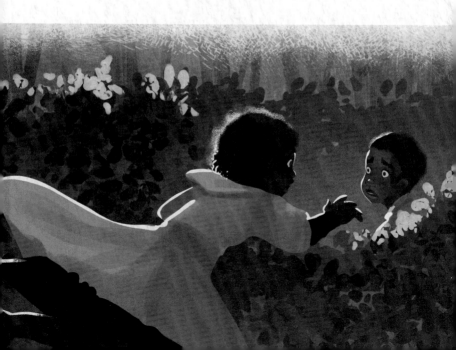

Suddenly more people than Ann could count came running out of the house. Ann could tell some of them were runaways, and some of them were slave catchers.

Baby Elizabeth started to holler, so Mama nursed her to keep her quiet. The men hadn't heard the baby over all of the screaming.

Ann couldn't bear to watch what was happening, and she didn't want Paul to see it. She pulled Paul close and covered both of their faces. She felt Mama lay down in the bushes next to them. Tears stung Ann's eyes, even though they were pressed against her sleeve.

"Get him!" someone yelled.

"He went that way," said another voice.

Ann had no idea how many of the slaves had been caught, but she heard the wagon leave. After a while, the night was quiet again. The only sound was Mama trying not to make noise while she cried.

They waited until the moon was high in the sky, but Daddy never came back.

Finally Mama whispered, "We have to go back."

"To the river?" asked Paul.

"No," said Mama. "We have to go back home to the farm. We can't go on without Daddy."

Ann knew going home was a mistake. Their only hope of survival was ahead of them—not behind them. That meant she would have to lead her family to the North. She would have to be a conductor on the Underground Railroad.

CHAPTER SIX

Ann couldn't let Mama give up on their freedom. She couldn't let Paul down. She couldn't let baby Elizabeth grow up and spend her whole life working in a field for nothing.

"Let's go on," Ann whispered. They had to keep moving. She led them back to the river, right into the water.

Mama put a hand on Ann's shoulder to make her stop. "We have to go back, Ann."

Paul started to cry. "They're gon' sell us, Mama. I don't want to be sold."

"Shh," said Mama. "Someone will hear you carrying on."

Everyone being upset made Elizabeth cry, and Ann got angry. "You two are going to get us killed. If we go back, there's no telling what they'll do. If we stand here, we'll get caught for sure," she said. "You all need to hush. We're going north."

Ann was surprised by the strength in her words. She didn't usually talk to her Mama like this. Paul looked up at Mama, who blinked and stared at Ann.

Mama put her finger in Elizabeth's mouth, and the baby stopped crying. Paul wiped his tears with his hand. They looked ready to move on.

Ann nodded and continued in the direction Daddy had told them to go. She made them walk all night long. She wanted to get as far away from that house and those pattyrollers as she could.

Finally the river started to narrow, and Ann stopped. "We'll rest here."

"Ann, I can't do this alone," said Mama, starting to cry again. "Not with the baby and the two of you."

Ann said, "Mama, you're not alone. You have me."

Mama sighed. "It would be bad to go back," she said. "Are you sure you want to do this without Daddy?"

Ann didn't know if it was fear or hope—or the promise she'd made to Daddy after Elizabeth was born—that made her so determined. She *would* keep her family safe. Ann nodded, and she knew that settled it. Their journey north wasn't over yet.

Mama opened her pouch of food. There wasn't much left. Just a few strips of pork, two pieces of ashcake, and a few little carrots. She ate carrots and a piece of pork, then gave the rest to Ann and Paul. Ann would have to figure out how to get them more food when they moved on.

Paul broke the silence. "Where's Daddy?" he asked.

It was the question Ann had been asking herself. She knew Mama was thinking about Daddy too. Even though Ann wanted to know, she was afraid to find out. The combination of thinking about Daddy and sitting in the cold night in wet clothes made her shiver.

"I don't know," said Mama. "I hope he got away. My heart can't take losing anybody else in this family." Fresh tears rolled down her cheeks, and her shoulders slumped. Mama looked like she was too tired to hold her own head up.

Ann knew Mama was thinking about Granny. She spotted some logs not too far off and helped Mama lay down behind one of them. "Get some rest," Ann whispered.

Mama lay on her side and nursed Elizabeth. Ann put Paul behind another log. She lay with him until he started to snore, then she crept off to her own log. She needed to be alone to think.

Ann didn't know she'd fallen asleep until the barking of bloodhounds woke her up. In a single movement, she was on her feet. She rushed to Mama and helped her up. Paul grabbed Mama's hand.

Deep barks, growls, and howls echoed through the night. The dogs sounded like they wanted nothing more than to catch Ann and her family. Ann wanted nothing more than to make sure that didn't happen.

"Run!" said Ann.

It was still dark, but Ann could see the river. She didn't want to run in it, because the dogs would hear the splashing. But if they didn't run in the river, they would leave footprints.

Ann knew their footprints would give the dogs a scent to follow. So she did the only thing she could think of. She ran as close to the river as she could without being in it.

As she ran, she kept looking back to see if Mama and Paul were still with her. Mama and Paul held hands and pulled each other along. The sling that held Elizabeth was cradled in Mama's other hand. She was trying to keep Elizabeth from bouncing.

Ann heard the dogs splashing in the river behind them. They were getting closer. She would have to try to confuse them. Even though Ann knew it would make noise, she ran into the river hoping they wouldn't leave a scent for the dogs to follow. After a while she slowed down.

Silently Ann mouthed, *We have to cross.* She pointed to the other side of the river.

Paul's eyes got wide, and he shook his head. Ann walked back to Paul and put him on her back. He was heavier than he looked. She started across the river, and Mama walked right next to her. Ann tested the bed of the river before each step she took.

She didn't want to fall. If it got deep suddenly, she would drop Paul. Ann couldn't swim. They would both drown.

When the water was up to their waists, Ann started to panic. She had no idea how deep the river was. She took deep breaths to help herself stay calm as the barking of the bloodhounds grew more frantic. Soon the water was so high Mama had to raise Elizabeth up. Paul's behind was in the water.

One of the dogs let out a long howl, and Ann could see a spot of light far off in the distance. The men were catching up.

Just when Ann thought they were going to have to head back the way they came, the river got shallow again, and they made it out on the other side. Ann began to run. She forgot to watch for the North Star. She ran like their lives depended on it.

CHAPTER **SEVEN**

Behind her, Ann could hear the dogs barking.
Then she heard a man shout. "Which way did they
go?" he yelled.

She kept running. When Ann looked back
to make sure Mama and Paul were keeping up,
Mama was limping. She didn't seem like she would
make it much farther.

Ann searched the land around them for a place
to hide. Their choices were to run toward the trees
or to run toward a farm in the distance.

Ann's mind raced. If she ran into the woods, they might go too far off their path and get lost. But running toward the farm meant running toward people. And those people might capture them. But the men would probably think they ran into the trees, because it wouldn't make sense for runaways to run to a stranger's house.

So Ann headed to the farm with Mama, baby Elizabeth, and Paul right behind her. When she reached the fence, she saw she was next to a pigpen. There was a mama pig with a few babies.

The mama raised her head and stared at Ann. Ann didn't want to make the pigs squeal and give away their location, so she went around to the other side of the pen. She found a pile of wood there.

Ann motioned for her family to sit between the wood and the pen. Once they were all on the ground, she covered as much of their bodies as she could with wood.

As her breathing slowed, Ann heard the dogs getting closer. Then she heard one of the men whistle and yell at them, and they changed direction. The dogs knew where Ann's family was hiding, but the men didn't believe they went to the farm. They had called their dogs away. Ann's trick had worked.

Paul wiggled under the wood. "Be still, Paul," said Ann.

"Are the dogs gone?" asked Paul.

Ann nodded. She looked at Mama. Silent tears fell from Mama's closed eyes. Her lips moved. Ann knew Mama was praying.

They lay like that until the sun came up. Shortly after sunrise, Ann heard footsteps coming from the direction of the house.

"Here, pigs," said a man's voice.

The pigs snorted at the man, and Ann heard what sounded like mud splashing, which was a sound she was too familiar with now. At first she wasn't sure what the sound was, then she realized the man had just poured breakfast for the pigs.

Ann knew pigs ate people food. She waited until she was positive the man was gone but not long enough for the pigs to eat their meal.

"Stay here," she whispered to Mama and Paul.

Ann snuck back around the pen. She crawled to the fence next to the pig trough. The food smelled good.

She reached through the fence, but the mama pig snapped at her. Ann drew her hand back and moved to the side of the trough where the piglets were. The mama pig watched her.

As quick as a snake Ann's hand went in, grabbed a fistful of food, and pulled back out. She used her skirt to hold the food and took as many fistfuls as she could until the mama pig tried to bite her.

Ann cradled the food in her skirt and crawled back to Mama and Paul. They all lay on their stomachs and ate the slops. There were chunks of cornbread, yams, ham scraps, and apple peels.

It reminded Ann of their Saturday night gatherings, and she realized the pigs ate better than she usually did. But for now, she was just happy to have food. Ann had managed to steal enough from the pigs to fill their stomachs.

When they had just finished, Elizabeth started to cry. Mama tried to nurse her, but she wouldn't eat. Mama tried sticking her finger in Elizabeth's mouth, but the baby pushed it back out with her tongue. Finally Mama put her hand over Elizabeth's mouth. Nothing worked. The pigs started to squeal.

Across the farm a man shouted, "David, go see about those pigs!"

"Yessir," said a voice that Ann figured must be David.

Quickly Ann, Mama, and Paul buried themselves in as much wood as they could before David arrived.

"What's the matter with you?" David asked the pigs.

A piglet made a high-pitched sound. So did Elizabeth. David heard it. "That wasn't no pig," he said.

Ann could tell David was walking toward them. She knew they were going to get caught, because Elizabeth would not be quiet. Ann could just see the top of David's head from where she was. Soon she saw his dark brown face peering down at them. He gasped.

"You stay right there," he said. "Don't you move. I'mma send somebody down here to help you."

Then David hurried away shouting, "Those greedy pigs are fighting over the slops!"

In a few minutes a very old woman arrived at the woodpile. Her face was more wrinkled than anyone's Ann had ever seen. "Come on," she whispered.

They followed the woman to a row of cabins. They were just like the cabins the slaves lived in back home. The woman took them inside of one. She didn't speak at all. She lit the cook fire and motioned for them to sit. Then she disappeared.

Ann said, "Mama, why is Elizabeth crying so much?"

"I don't think I have enough milk," said Mama.

"Why?" asked Paul.

"I just don't," said Mama. She said it in a way that meant she was done talking about it.

Ann got closer to the fire and watched Mama try to feed Elizabeth.

"Mama, we're never going to make it if Elizabeth keeps crying," said Ann.

Mama looked at Ann with worried eyes.

"I know," she said. After a while, Elizabeth dozed off, and Mama handed her to Paul. Then she untied and slipped off the shoes that Mattie had given her.

Ann's breath caught in her throat. Mama's feet were red and blistered. "What's wrong with your feet?" she asked.

Mama said, "It's these shoes."

Ann realized that Mama had been limping not because she was tired but because her feet were hurt. Ann thought shoes were supposed to make walking easier, not harder.

The cabin felt so familiar that Ann fell asleep and slept the whole day away. When she woke up, the sun had gone down, and a woman Ann didn't recognize was making dinner.

The wrinkled old lady was back, and she was sewing near the fire. David waited by the fire for dinner.

When dinner was ready the younger woman served David first. He held her hand for a moment after she handed him his food. Ann could tell she was David's wife. Next she served Ann's family, the old woman, and herself.

"Eat," said David. "Then we'll talk."

Mama opened her mouth to speak, but David put up his hand. "Eat first" he said. "Don't even tell me your name. The less we know, the better."

The old woman began to sing a song about Moses leading the slaves from Egypt. Every now and then she'd stop long enough to eat some grits. All six of them ate without talking. Ann wondered what David wanted to talk about.

Finally he spoke. "You must be lost," he said.

"We are," said Paul. "My daddy's lost too."

"Shhh," said Mama.

David, his wife, and the old woman looked at each other.

Elizabeth started crying like the thought of her lost daddy made her sad. The old woman took her from Mama. She pinched some grits with two fingers, blew on them, and put them in Elizabeth's mouth. Ann thought Mama was going to have a fit, but the baby stopped crying and Mama looked relieved.

The wife finished her dinner and then worked on Mama's feet. Elizabeth ate more grits from the older woman's fingers. Paul finished his food and laid his head in Mama's lap. Ann was proud she'd done the right thing by running to the farm.

David waited for a quiet to settle over the cabin, then he said, "The next station ain't too far from here. I'll tell you the way."

Ann couldn't believe her luck. None of the slaves at her farm knew where the stations were. She wanted to ask David how he knew, but she didn't. She paid attention to every detail and by the time they left the cabin, she knew exactly where to go.

CHAPTER **EIGHT**

Eastern Maryland, further north along the Choptank River
Tuesday, November 21, 1854
Late evening

Ann thanked the three people for their help.
Mama had decided to leave the shoes behind and
wore fresh wraps around her feet. She had a bundle
full of food for them to eat, and baby Elizabeth was
sleeping with her mouth open.

Without a word, Mama fell to the back and let
Ann lead the way. Ann led her family to the woods
beyond the farm. It was too cloudy to see the North
Star, so Ann followed David's advice. He had told
her moss only grew on the north side of the trees
and that could help her stay on track.

Halfway through the night, Paul started complaining. "Slow down," he said.

Ann glared at him. "Do you want to make it to the station before light?"

Paul pouted, but he didn't complain again, and they kept a steady pace. Since they'd just eaten a good meal, they didn't even stop to eat. Finally they came to a white house with a candle burning in one window. It was just like David had said.

Ann thought about what had happened at the last house that was supposed to be a station. That mistake may have cost Daddy his life. She stood and looked at the house for quite some time. She was losing her nerve.

"Are we going in?" asked Paul. He had the loudest whisper Ann had ever heard.

"Shhh," said Mama. Her face was full of doubt.

Finally Ann knew she would have to move forward, even though she was uncertain. She took a deep breath and headed to the door with her family behind her. She knocked three times, just like David had told her to.

A woman's voice said, "Who's there?"

Ann used the code David had given her. "A friend with friends," she said.

The door opened, and a pale woman ushered them in. A pale man sat in a chair near the fire. He stood up and came to introduce himself.

"I'm Donovan," he said. "This is my wife, Sally."

Sally said, "Please, sit and rest over there." She pointed to the chairs near the fire.

Ann had never been inside a white person's house. She'd never had white people treat her like this. She wanted to trust them, but she had no reason to. She smiled politely and sat down. But she positioned herself so that if they had to run, she could get her family out quickly.

Donovan sat down with them, and Sally disappeared through a door to the left of the fire. Before long she returned and led them through the same door. Inside was a real bed covered with a nice warm blanket. Ann thought it must be where Sally and Donovan slept.

Sally had water ready for them to wash up and fresh clothes for them to wear. The clothes were much nicer than anything Ann's family had ever owned, and they fit.

After they changed, Sally gave them warm soup and fresh bread to eat. The bread was so good Ann wanted more, but she was afraid to ask.

"First, you'll rest," said Donovan. "Then I'll put you in the wagon and take you to the next station."

"How long until we're in the North?" Mama asked Donovan.

"You should cross the Mason-Dixon Line into Pennsylvania in two days," said Donovan.

Ann didn't understand what any of this meant. "Is Pennsylvania the North?" she asked.

Donovan nodded. "It is," he said. "You will find many people like yourselves there."

After they finished eating, Sally led them to the barn. At the far end there was an area with a large amount of straw.

"You will rest here," said Sally. "Donovan will come for you at dawn."

"We're traveling during the day?" asked Ann. She didn't think that was a good idea. Daddy had warned her against it.

"Yes," said Sally. "But don't worry. Donovan will keep you safe."

Mama said, "Miss Sally, thank you for everything you've done for us."

Sally smiled, but she had a sad look in her eyes. "It is the right thing to do. No one should be a slave," she said. "You must stay quiet now."

The next morning, Donovan helped them into a wagon. He carefully arranged potatoes all around them, even on top. Then he covered them and the potatoes with a big cloth. A small amount of light filtered through, and Ann focused on the faces of her family. It helped keep her calm.

They bumped along in the back of the wagon all day. Ann wished she could see where they were going, but she knew better than to take a peek.

Later in the day, the wagon slowed down. Then it came to a complete stop. Ann hoped that meant they were at the station.

Suddenly a deep voice said, "We're looking for some runaways."

Pattyrollers, thought Ann. They were not at the next station yet.

She heard Donovan say, "I haven't seen anyone running."

"It's a family," said the deep voice. "A mother, a father, and three kids. One is a baby."

Ann's heart thudded in her chest. People were searching for them, but they didn't know Daddy wasn't with them. Paul's eyes were wide, and Ann could tell he was about to say something. She put her hand over his mouth.

"I haven't seen them," said Donovan.

It was hard for Ann to believe that Donovan was telling a lie to keep them safe. Daddy was right about good and bad coming in all colors. Donovan was putting himself in danger for them.

"What's in the wagon today?" asked the man.

"Potatoes," said Donovan.

Ann hoped the man would believe Donovan. They were so close to the North. They couldn't get caught now.

"Mind if I take a look?" asked the voice.

At that moment, Ann spotted a spider! It was a large brown spider, almost the color of the potatoes. It crawled toward her face. She looked at Mama and tried to get her to notice the spider, but Mama was too busy watching the baby.

A scream was building in Ann's throat. The spider was getting closer. In a minute, it would be on her face. A squeak so quiet you'd have to be lying next to her to hear it escaped from Ann.

Donovan said, "Sure, you can take a look."

The spider inched closer. Ann heard the pattyroller's footsteps walking around to the back of the wagon. She also heard another wagon approaching.

The pattyroller lifted a small corner of the cloth that hid them. It let in just enough light for Ann to see the spider's eyes. The spider froze in the light. Ann and the spider stared at each other as the cloth rose higher.

Be brave, Ann said to herself over and over again. *Be brave.*

CHAPTER **NINE**

Ann held her breath and prayed the spider would turn around and go the other way. She still had one hand over Paul's mouth. The other hand was buried under the potatoes. If she uncovered Paul's mouth she could smash the spider, but if she did that, the pattyroller might see her move, and Paul might let out a scream.

The other wagon came to a stop behind theirs. A voice Ann hadn't heard yet said, "Hey, Tom. What you got there?"

Tom said, "I'm about to find out."

He lifted the cloth higher, and Ann heard a few potatoes tumble onto the ground. One of the horses spooked. Ann heard shuffling and pawing, and a horse whinnied. The cloth dropped back down as the men outside struggled to calm the frightened horse.

Ann watched in horror as the spider started moving toward her face again. Then Mama's hand came down on the spider, squishing it just before it reached Ann's face.

"Whoa!" yelled a voice. "Calm down, old boy!"

Tom's deep voice said, "This horse is scared of everything." Then he yelled toward Donovan, "You can go on."

The wagon lurched forward, and they were on their way again. Ann, Mama, and Paul all let out big sighs. They'd been holding their breath. Baby Elizabeth had slept through the whole thing.

The rest of the day was quiet, and they reached the next station at nightfall. Donovan lifted the cover and moved the potatoes off Ann and her family. They had parked at the back of a building with a pointed roof.

Mama sighed. "Good, a church."

Ann and her family climbed down from the wagon and looked up at the dark shape of the church.

Donovan said, "I have to get back now."

"Thank you for helping us," said Mama. She paused for a moment. "Do you think you can find out what happened to my husband, John?"

"I will try," said Donovan. The doors at the back of the church opened, and two men came out to greet them.

One was tall and pale, with a gray beard. The other was a much shorter dark-skinned man. The man with the beard said, "Come with us."

As Donovan rode away on his wagon, they went inside and the smaller man closed the church doors behind them. The two men led them through a small chapel and up a narrow staircase into the bell tower.

"The space in the tower is small," said the man with the beard, "but it is big enough to hide in." The bell tower reminded Ann of a big wooden bird's nest.

There were no introductions. Donovan had told them before they left his home not to give out their names. He said it made it easier for people to say, "I haven't met anyone named Beth," if they were questioned.

The man with the beard said, "You'll eat and sleep here tonight." Then he gestured toward the shorter man. "Tomorrow, Melvin will take you into Pennsylvania."

Ann's heart leapt. They were only a day away
from freedom. Although she was full of excitement,
she was also curious about how Melvin would
be able to take them across the state line. Melvin
had brown skin. Surely a Negro man would catch
someone's attention.

"How is he going to do that?" asked Ann.

Melvin grinned. "You'll see."

Ann was beginning to realize there were a
lot of good people in the world outside the farm.
She was learning there were people who could be
trusted. She decided to let herself sleep and wait for
tomorrow.

Northern Maryland, just south of the Mason-Dixon Line
Thursday, November 23, 1854
Sunrise

The next morning, a young woman came into
the church. She brought ham, eggs, and bread for

their breakfast. She also brought *very* fancy clothes. Ann had only seen clothes this fine once in her life, when two guests came to the farm to do business with Master Adam. There were lots of whispers in the field that day about the rich guests who came to visit.

"Put on these clothes," said the young woman. "Melvin will be here shortly."

Mama looked at the expensive clothes. "Oh, we can't take those," she said.

The woman smiled. "Yes, you can. We have lots of friends who help us with disguises and food and even money," she said. Before she left she added, "Good luck."

Ann slipped into a white dress, and Mama helped with the buttons in the back. Once Ann was dressed, she didn't even feel like herself. The dress was heavy on her body, and the bonnet was uncomfortable.

Mama looked beautiful in her long, blue dress. Paul wore nice black pants, and Elizabeth had a little white gown. The young woman helped them lace up their fancy shoes.

Ann thought these clothes were just right for her family to wear as they crossed the line into freedom.

Melvin met them at the door. He was dressed up too. "We'll pretend I'm your husband," he said to Mama.

Mama looked horrified. "I have a hus—" she started to say. When she stopped, Ann wondered if it was because there was no way to know if Mama still had a husband or not.

Melvin didn't wait for Mama to finish. He said, "It's just for show. I'm free. You'll be my pretend family, and people will think you're free too. We'll ride in a wagon like everyone else."

Paul asked, "Out in the open?"

Melvin said, "Hiding in plain sight."

Ann didn't think the plan would work. Negroes didn't dress like this. It would just make people suspicious. She thought Donovan's way was better. They needed to hide or travel at night. Ann had not forgotten that she was the conductor for her family.

"Melvin, we don't want to get caught," said Ann. "I don't like this idea."

"Ann!" said Mama. "Don't be rude."

Melvin interrupted. "Do you know how many families have ridden in my wagon?"

Ann shook her head.

"Nine," said Melvin.

Ann still thought it was a bad idea. She had learned already that things on the journey to freedom didn't always go as planned. But if she wanted to get her family to freedom, she would have to take a chance.

They all climbed into the wagon. Ann and Mama adjusted their bonnets so most of their faces were covered. Mama held the newspaper Melvin gave her. She was supposed to read it if anyone gave them trouble.

Mama had said, "I can't read."

"Just pretend to read it," Melvin had told her. "Seeing you browse the pages will make people think you're free, since they won't teach slaves to read. It's all for show, remember?"

Ann and her family bounced along in the wagon. It was a nice change to travel during the day. Now Ann could see this new place where Negroes wore fancy clothes and sat in wagons. She was amazed by what she saw around her.

A Negro man passed them on the road in his own wagon and waved to Melvin. They arrived at a small town, and Melvin stopped the wagon.

"Why are you stopping?" asked Mama.

"You'll see," said Melvin. "Read the paper while I go inside."

Mama held the paper up to her face. Melvin turned the newspaper around the right way for Mama and disappeared into a little building. Ann held her head down but peeked out from under her bonnet.

Several Negro people walked through the town. They walked in and out of the buildings. Ann thought they must be close to the North if people were being this bold. No one looked afraid.

Melvin came back and handed them each a molasses cookie. Paul took a big bite. "Mmmmm!" he said.

Ann nibbled on the cookie. It was the most delicious thing she'd ever tasted. As the wagon continued on its journey, Ann ate her cookie as slowly as possible. She wanted to make it last.

Eventually Paul fell asleep, and his head bounced against Ann's arm. At sunset, Melvin stopped the wagon again.

"Congratulations," said Melvin. "We just crossed the Mason-Dixon Line. You're free."

Mama began to weep. "We're in the North?" she asked.

Melvin nodded. "Yes, Ma'am."

Ann smiled. *I led my family to freedom,* she thought to herself. Then she realized she had no idea what they were supposed to do next. Daddy hadn't said anything about their future in the North. Now Daddy wasn't here to tell them how to survive. They had no place to live. They had no money and no jobs. They didn't even know any people.

Melvin interrupted her thoughts. "Now remember," he said, "some people may still be looking to capture you and take you back, so you need to be careful."

The molasses cookie tried to work its way up Ann's throat. She hadn't expected freedom to be scary.

CHAPTER TEN

Ann had not prepared herself for freedom.
She hadn't thought about anything but getting to
the North. Now they were going to be dropped off
and left to figure out freedom without Daddy.

Melvin said, "Climb on down."

"Out of the wagon?" asked Ann.

"Yes," he said.

Ann said, "You're leaving us here?"

Melvin laughed. "No!" he said. "But don't you
want to put your feet on free land?"

They all climbed out of the wagon and stood in the North. The North was fancy clothes and tight shoes and not forgetting people might be looking for you. The North was a place without Daddy. But the North was also molasses cookies and freedom and no slave owners or overseers.

Paul jumped up and down. He turned in a circle and clapped his hands. Paul, who was afraid of everything, was the only one who didn't seem afraid.

A wagon approached, and Mama looked at Melvin with a worried expression.

"Don't worry," he said. "We're trading wagons. The horses need a break."

A man with bright blue eyes and dark clothes climbed down, shook Melvin's hand, and left again in Melvin's wagon.

"How did he know we were here?" Ann asked.

Melvin winked. "I sent a message from town."

Ann realized Melvin must have done this when he bought the cookies. She smiled at him.

"All right," said Melvin. "Climb back in. I'm going to take you to Philadelphia."

"What's in Philadelphia?" asked Ann.

"People who will help you get used to your freedom," he said.

Philadelphia, Pennsylvania
Friday, November 24, 1854
After midnight

By the time they got to Philadelphia, it was the middle of the night. Melvin led them to a large house. Ann could hear people talking and laughing inside. Melvin knocked on the door.

A woman who reminded Ann of a younger version of Granny answered. "Welcome. I'm Gloria," she said. She led them through the hall. "It's a busy night. Another man just got here too."

They followed Gloria into a bright kitchen. A man sat at the table with his back to them. He was slumped over his food, eating like he was starving and exhausted at the same time.

Delicious smells of yams and ham filled Ann's nose. She thought about the pigs and their slops. This time she'd be eating her own food as a free girl.

Gloria motioned to the table. "Go ahead and sit down," she said. "I'll fix you some plates."

Paul was the first one at the table. He plopped down next to the man. "Hello," he said to the man.

The man's head snapped up. "Paul?"

"Daddy!" yelled Paul.

Paul jumped up so fast he knocked his chair over. Ann and Mama rushed over, and they all stood in the middle of the kitchen with their arms wrapped around each other. Mama laughed and cried and rubbed Daddy's back. Ann breathed in the comforting smell of dirt and Daddy's sweat.

Daddy asked, "How did you get here?"

Mama said, "We had our own conductor." She winked at Ann and smiled.

Daddy squeezed Ann so hard her feet left the floor. "I knew I could count on you."

"I remembered to be brave," said Ann. "Looks like you did too, Daddy."

They all laughed and sat down to eat their first meal together as a free family. Now Ann didn't have to *imagine* eating at a real table together. And she didn't have to worry about getting sold. She watched Mama, who told Daddy all about their journey. It was more talking than Mama had done in two months.

As she watched her reunited family, Ann knew everything would be all right. Anyone who had survived slavery and a journey on the Underground Railroad could certainly figure out freedom.

A NOTE FROM THE AUTHOR

The institution of slavery was one of the most shameful practices in history. In the United States, millions of Africans and African Americans were enslaved over a period of more than two hundred years. Even the very young and old were forced into slavery.

Enslaved people worked long and difficult hours six to seven days a week for no money, little food, and poor living conditions. In addition to this, enslaved people were often beaten and otherwise cruelly treated. People were considered property and were bought and sold. Often families were separated and sold to different owners.

It's no wonder enslaved people found ways to escape. One such way became known as the Underground Railroad. The name is misleading. As Ann says, it wasn't under the ground and it had nothing to do with trains.

Slaves used the word *underground* because it could not be seen. The routes, paths, and "stations" were kept secret to avoid getting caught. *Railroad* refers to the fact that a route was followed with stops along the way, just like a train.

The Underground Railroad helped enslaved people run away from "slave states" in the South, where slavery was allowed. Their destination was "free states" in the North, where slavery was not legal. In most instances, even those in charge of the stations did not know the entire route. This ensured that if a station was discovered or if people were caught, no one would be able to give away the rest of the stations or put other people in danger. The high level of secrecy and organization is part of what made it so successful.

The conductors were the people who led runaways to the North and kept them safe. The most famous conductor on the Underground Railroad was Harriet Tubman. There are disagreements about how many enslaved people she helped become free, but some say she helped as many as 300 people. She risked her life at least nineteen times, returning to the South to rescue enslaved people and lead them to the North.

Harriet Tubman was born in Maryland in 1820 and lived her life there as a slave until she ran away in 1849. Most of her trips on the Underground Railroad were between Maryland and as far north as Canada.

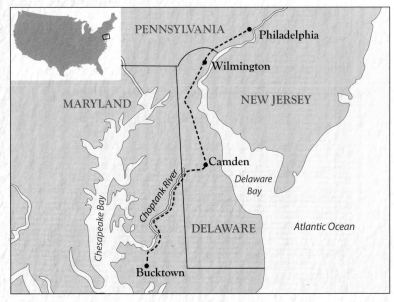

Although Harriet Tubman's own escape route is unknown, experts believe she traveled along the Choptank River and through Delaware to Pennsylvania.

The routes she used are some of the best documented, and there is now a Harriet Tubman Museum and Educational Center in Maryland. The Harriet Tubman Scenic Byway and Visitor Center are part of the National Historic Park in Maryland. These are some of the reasons I chose to start Ann's journey there.

Although the Underground Railroad was highly organized, it was both formal and informal. Some runaways had a conductor. Others left with no conductor and no knowledge of where the stations were. They followed the North Star and other clues on their journey. They were part of the Underground Railroad too.

Whether there was a conductor or not, the trip was challenging and dangerous. People travelled at night through unfamiliar territory with no roads. They often left on a Saturday night, because if they had Sunday off, no one would miss them until Monday. Ads and wanted signs for runaways could not be placed over the weekend. This gave them a head start. Runaways were hunted by slave catchers and patrollers (pattyrollers) who were willing to hurt them. If they were caught and returned to their "owners," they were severely punished.

The Fugitive Slave Act of 1850 required that even former slaves who made it to a free state had to be returned if caught. The story *Ann Fights for Freedom* takes place in 1854, during the time of Harriet Tubman, the Underground Railroad, and The Fugitive Slave Act. Even though it isn't a true story, many of the things that happened to Ann and her family happened to real people.

When I wrote this story I had three goals. I wanted to tell a realistic and accurate story, yet still write a book that children could enjoy. I wanted to show many different kinds of people working together to lead enslaved people to freedom and to fight for equality. My third goal was to write a suspenseful story about a girl who didn't give up and led her family to freedom.

I hope this story makes you hold your breath and cross your fingers for Ann. I also hope you learn a bit about history. Maybe you will work with others to fight for what you think is right. Maybe YOU will be an everyday hero too.

MAKING CONNECTIONS

1. List three character traits that Ann possesses. Then choose one and write a paragraph that includes examples of how Ann shows this trait in the story.

2. The climax of a book is when the tension or action reaches its highest point. What scene do you think is the climax of this book? Explain your answer.

3. Baby Elizabeth will not remember her family's journey north. Pretend you are Ann and write her a letter telling her about it.

GLOSSARY

ashcake (ASH-kayk)—cake made out of cornmeal that is cooked in hot ashes

conductor (kuhn-DUHK-tur)—people who guided runaway slaves and led them to the free states in the North

embers (EM-burz)—hot, glowing remains of a fire

grits (GRITS)—coarsely ground grain, especially white corn, boiled and eaten as a cereal or side dish

hog jowls (HOG JOULS)—a cured and smoked cut of meat from the cheeks of a hog

Mason-Dixon Line (MAY-suhn DIK-suhn LINE)—boundary line between Pennsylvania and Maryland; was in part boundary between free and slave states

mouth harp (MOUTH HARP)—an instrument consisting of a flexible metal or bamboo tongue or reed attached to a frame

overseer (OH-ver-see-er)—person who directed the daily work of slaves

rations (RASH-uhns)—limited amounts or shares, especially of food

slavery (SLAY-vuh-ree)—the practice of owning people and thinking of them as property

Underground Railroad (UHN-dur-ground RAYL-rohd)—a network of people who secretly helped slaves from the South escape to free states in the North or to Canada before the American Civil War

ABOUT THE AUTHOR

Nikki Shannon Smith is from Oakland, California, but she now lives in the Central Valley with her husband and two children. She has worked in elementary education for more than 25 years, and writes everything from picture books to young adult novels. When she's not busy with family, work, or writing, she loves to visit the coast. The first thing she packs in her suitcase is always a book.